and the
Ballet Scheme

MONICA BROWN

and the
Ballet Scheme

ILLUSTRATED BY
Angela Dominguez

LITTLE, BROWN AND COMPANY
New York • Boston

Little, Brown and Company

Hachette Book Group
1290 Avenue of the Americas, New York, NY 10104
Visit us at lb-kids.com

Little, Brown and Company is a division of Hachette Book Group, Inc.
The Little, Brown name and logo are trademarks of Hachette Book Group, Inc.

First Edition: July 2016

Library of Congress Cataloging-in-Publication Data
Names: Brown, Monica, 1969– author. | Dominguez, Angela, illustrator.
Title: Lola Levine and the ballet scheme / by Monica Brown ; illustrated by Angela Dominguez.
Description: First edition. | New York : Little, Brown and Company, 2016. | Series: Lola Levine ; 3 |
Summary: "A new girl has joined Lola Levine's second-grade class. When they get off on the wrong foot, they are forced to spend time together...and learn they have more in common than they thought"— Provided by publisher.
Identifiers: LCCN 2015034864| ISBN 9780316258449 (hardback) | ISBN 9780316258456 (ebook)
Subjects: | CYAC: Friendship—Fiction. | Difference (Psychology)—Fiction. | Ballet dancing—Fiction. | Soccer—Fiction. | Jews—United States—Fiction. | Hispanic Americans—Fiction. | BISAC: JUVENILE FICTION / Family / Parents. | JUVENILE FICTION / Family / Siblings. | JUVENILE FICTION / People & Places / United States / Hispanic & Latino. | JUVENILE FICTION / Religious / Jewish.
Classification: LCC PZ7.B816644 Loc 2016 | DDC [Fic]—dc23 LC record available at
http://lccn.loc.gov/2015034864

10 9 8 7 6 5 4 3 2 1

RRD-C

Printed in the United States of America

For super best friends Shannon, Mary, Annette, Leilah, Michelle, Lisa, Shawn, and Carrie, of course

CONTENTS

Chapter One

Chapter Two

Chapter Three

Chapter Four

Dear *Diario*,

During class today, I noticed
that Makayla Miller, Alyssa
Goldstein, and Olivia Lopez all
had the same nail polish on. It
seemed like every girl in my class
did. They were whispering, but
I heard them talking about a
slumber party. I've never been to
a slumber party, or even been
invited to one.

I like nail polish, too. I use it
for what my dad calls "creative
expression." When I have a soccer
game, I paint my nails orange
to match my uniform. When I'm
happy, I sometimes paint my nails

1

all the colors of the rainbow.
Once, when I was sad, I used a
permanent marker to draw frown
faces on each finger, but Mom
said that wasn't a good idea at
all. How was I supposed to know
that permanent marker was, well,
permanent?

I'm glad I have soccer practice
tomorrow because soccer always
makes me feel better.

Shalom,
Lola Levine

Chapter One
The New Girl

"I wonder where Ms. Garcia is?" I ask Josh Blot as we walk into the second-grade classroom. Ms. Garcia is my favorite teacher ever. In fact, last week I wrote her an acrostic saying just that:

Magnificent
Smart

Great
Awesome
Respectful
Cool
I can't think of a word that
begins with I
Amazing

A poem is acrostic when each letter of a word begins each line in the poem. Guess who taught me that? Ms. Garcia! I taught my brother, Ben, how to write an acrostic, but I sure didn't like his very much.

Loud voice
Ogre

Large ears
Afraid of me on the
soccer field

Mom didn't like it, either.

"Words are powerful," she told Ben. Mom is a journalist for the newspaper, so she knows words are pretty important. She sat down with Ben, and they made another acrostic for me.

Lovely
Orange Smoothies
Soccer team
Lively
Afraid of me on
the soccer field (just
kidding)

That's my brother.

"I saw Ms. Garcia in the front office talking to my mom and some girl I don't know," says Josh. I sure hope that Ms. Garcia isn't in trouble. I usually am when I talk to Josh's mom. Josh is my best friend, but his mom is the principal. I seem to get in trouble with Principal Blot a lot.

Ms. Garcia walks into our classroom just as the bell is ringing. She is not alone. She is walking next to a girl I've never seen before. The first thing I notice is that the girl is dressed in pink from head to toe. She has pink ribbons in her hair, a sweatshirt with pink slippers on it, and a skirt that looks sort of fluffy. Even her tennis shoes are pink! Her hair is long and black like my mom's, and her eyes are brown like mine.

"Class," Ms. Garcia says, "I'd like to introduce you to Isabella Benitez, a new member of our class. Make sure you make Isabella feel welcome today!"

"Ms. Garcia," the new girl says, "would you mind calling me Bella?"

"Of course not, Bella," says Ms. Garcia. "You can sit here, between Lola and Alyssa." Ms. Garcia always makes sure there's at least one seat between Alyssa and me because we bug each other so much. Now the new girl sits between us.

"Hi," says Alyssa, waving her hand. Bella waves back.

"I'm Lola!" I say, and she turns toward me.

"Lola is short for Dolores. My mom is from Peru—is yours, too? Do you speak Spanish? I do. My dad is from here. He's

Jewish. My mom's Catholic. I'm both. Do you play soccer? I do. Are those bedroom slippers on your sweatshirt? Do you always wear pink? Don't you get tired of it? It isn't a very interesting color, in my opinion—"

"Lola, be quiet!" Alyssa interrupts, rolling her eyes. "You'll get used to her," she says to Bella.

"Actually," Bella says, "these are ballet shoes, not bedroom slippers! And, for your information, pink is a *very* interesting color. It's the color of bubble gum and cotton candy and bunny eyes and—"

"It's also the color of my tongue," Alyssa says, sticking her tongue out at me.

"That's not nice, Alyssa!" I say loudly. Too loudly.

"Lola, please raise your hand if you have a question or comment," Ms. Garcia says.

"Sorry," I say, and try to sit quietly without fidgeting. Principal Blot once told me that I fidget too much. At first I didn't understand what she meant, but I learned pretty quickly that "fidget" is just a fancy word for wiggling, jiggling, and swinging my legs.

"I'm a soccer player," I explained to Principal Blot. "My legs like to move, even if I don't tell them to." I don't think she believed me.

I try to get Bella's attention again to tell her that I like cotton candy, too, but she stares straight ahead and doesn't look at me even once.

Chapter Two
Spirit Week

"Class, everyone's eyes on me," Ms. Garcia says, and we turn to the front of the room. "It's time to talk about Northland Elementary Spirit Week."

I raise my hand.

"Is that like Ghost Week? Can we have a haunted house?"

"No, Lola, Spirit Week celebrates school spirit. This is our twentieth year open as a school, and at the end of the month we are going to have all sorts of fun events. We are going to kick off the week with a school assembly and an ice-cream social, and each day we will dress up according to a different theme."

"Yeah!" the kids in my class say. I don't know what to think. I like the idea of ghosts better than dressing up.

Ms. Garcia goes to the board and writes:

Monday—Assembly and Ice-Cream Social
Tuesday—Mismatched Day

Wednesday—Pajama Day
Thursday—Tie-Dye Day
Friday—Twin Day

She turns back to the class and explains each day. I am especially excited about Mismatched Day because I think matching is boring. My mom once gave me a picture book called *Marisol McDonald Doesn't Match*, and I loved it so much. Marisol decided that she didn't care if people thought she was weird—she just wanted to be herself. I want to be myself, too, but I still want to be invited to slumber parties. When Ms. Garcia starts to talk about Pajama Day, I lean toward Bella.

"You can wear your bedroom slippers!" I say with a smile.

"They're ballet shoes, not bedroom slippers!" Bella says, and she doesn't smile back. What did I do wrong?

Ms. Garcia moves on to talk about Tie-Dye Day.

"What if we don't have a tie-dyed shirt?" Juan Gomez asks.

"That's part of the fun," says Ms. Garcia. "Our art project this Friday will be making tie-dyed T-shirts. Make sure to bring in a white T-shirt to school, and we will work on our Spirit Week shirts!"

Bella raises her hand.

"Can we tie-dye our T-shirts pink?" she asks.

"Yes," says Ms. Garcia, "you can pick the colors you like and mix new ones if we don't have them."

I'll do an orange tie-dye, of course, for

my soccer team, the Orange Smoothies. But I also love blue. And purple. I'm thinking about my design already.

I want to talk to Bella some more at recess, but just as I'm walking toward her, Makayla runs up and says, "I'm a dancer, too!" and drags her off. I don't care. I'd rather play soccer with Josh and Juan, anyway.

"Come on, Lola!" Juan says. "Josh and I are going to take shots on you."

"Do your best!" I say as I run toward the grass.

After school, I have soccer practice. Dad takes me because he's the assistant coach. He's a pretty fun coach.

"Remember, Smoothies, soccer is creative!" he says, and leads us in really fun warm-ups. We do Frankies and flamingos. With Frankies, we walk like a monster named Frankenstein with our arms out and our legs kicking straight ahead of us. For flamingos, we balance on one leg and hold our opposite ankle, pulling our foot toward our bottom. Flamingos are birds that sleep on one foot, which is very cool, in my opinion. Dad has animal names for most of our warm-ups—the inchworm, the bear, the seal. We laugh a lot during warm-ups.

Mr. Berg, our head coach, is a little tougher. He's always making us do dribbling and passing drills. I don't mind, though, because I love pretty much everything about soccer. After warm-ups, Coach Berg gathers us all together.

"Team, I have a few announcements," he says. "First, we need to really focus, because we are playing the Gray Sharks two weeks from Saturday, and they are the number one team in our league. If we win, we will be number one, and I know we can do it!"

"Yes, we can!" we yell.

"And even if we don't win, we'll do our best and have fun," my dad says. Coach Berg doesn't look like he agrees.

"My second announcement," Coach Berg goes on, "is that I've decided to have *two* co-captains this year. The first captain will continue to be Lola Levine, and her co-captain will be...Alyssa Goldstein."

What? I can't believe it! I mean, Alyssa is a good player, but she doesn't take soccer *seriously.*

"Congratulations, Alyssa," Coach Berg goes on. "I know you and Lola will work together to lead our team to victory!"

"And lead by being extra respectful and extra nice," Dad adds.

Later, when the team is practicing penalty shots, I stop Alyssa's fast shot to the left.

"That was just luck!" she says.

I'm about to tell Alyssa exactly what I think about that when I remember I'm a captain, and I'm supposed to be extra nice.

"Champions make their own luck" is what Alex Morgan would say. She plays on the US Olympic women's soccer team and is an amazing forward, in my opinion. I have lots of opinions, and one of them is that Alyssa Goldstein shouldn't be co-captain of the Orange Smoothies!

When I get home, I write a note to Dad and leave it wrapped around his paintbrush in his art studio. He likes to spend an hour in there after dinner.

Dear Dad:

Why did you choose Alyssa to be a co-captain? We couldn't

get along if we tried, and Alyssa won't try, that's for sure!

Shalom,
Your daughter
(Lola Levine)

That night, Dad tucks me in.

"Hey, Daughter Lola Levine," Dad says, holding my note. "Coach Berg and I thought making you co-captains might help you and Alyssa learn to work together. All I'm asking is that you give Alyssa a chance."

"Okay, Dad," I say, and try to smile.

"That's my girl!" Dad says, and wishes me a "very good night. I hope your dreams are filled with unicorns and balloons and soccer balls and doughnuts and—"

"All good things!" I interrupt. "I get it, Dad," I say with a real smile this time.

He turns out the light.

Chapter Three
Uh-Oh

Dear *Diario*,

Just a quick note to say, "Yay!"
We are tie-dyeing our T-shirts today
for Spirit Week, which is only two

weeks away! I have to remember to ask Josh what we are wearing for Twin Day. I think we should dress up as soccer players.

Dad just yelled up that breakfast is ready, so I've got to go.

Shalom,
Lola Levine

At breakfast, Ben makes a mess of his eggs, as usual, squirting ketchup designs all over his plate. Ben seems to think that ketchup and scrambled eggs go together. I disagree. I can't even see Ben's eggs under his mountain of ketchup.

"*Dolores*," Ben starts, "I need some advice."

I purposely ignore Ben when he calls
me by my full name. He knows I don't like
it, even if I'm named after my *tía* Dolores.
She goes by Lola, too.

"Okay," he says. "Lola. I need advice
about Pajama Day during Spirit Week."

"Why do you need advice?" I say. "Just

wear a pair of your pajamas. It's pretty easy."

"But what about Chewie?" Ben asks.

"What about him?" I say. Chewie is a really old and ugly worn-out teddy bear that Ben still sleeps with. He's missing an ear, and his paws don't match because Ben used to chew on them. Bubbe, my grandma Levine, patched Chewie's paws up so many times that the fur on each one is a different color brown. Ben finally stopped chewing on his teddy bear, but he still sleeps with him every single night.

"Well, for Pajama Day, we are supposed to dress in what we sleep in each night, and I sleep with Chewie every night. If he sees me in my pajamas and I leave him, his feelings will get hurt!"

"Chewie doesn't have feelings, Ben. Because he's a STUFFED ANIMAL," I say. "Don't bring that gross bear to school!"

"Lola," Mom says, "Ben has strong feelings about Chewie, and that's okay."

"And how do you know that Chewie doesn't have feelings, anyway!" Ben says. "He talks to me at night sometimes when I'm scared."

"Maybe in your dreams," I say, but Dad gives me a look.

"Having an imagination is important," Dad says. "And having a big imagination is great. But if you bring Chewie to school, Ben, then you might lose him."

"Oh," says Ben, who has ketchup smeared all over his face.

"And people might tease you," I say.

"Trust me, I know all about that." Dad gives me a pat on the back.

We get to school early, for once, and just before class starts, I run up to Josh.

"Hey!" I say. "What are we going to wear for Twin Day? I think we should wear our black soccer shorts and—"

"Lola," he interrupts, "we can't be twins."

"Why not?" I ask.

"Well, you're a girl—"

"I KNOW I'm a girl, Josh," I say grumpily, "but boys and girls can be twins."

"But...," says Josh.

"But?" I ask.

"I already told Juan I'd be his twin," Josh says.

"Fine," I say, and I'm glad when the bell finally rings.

During art class, Ms. Garcia explains our tie-dye project.

"We'll tie up our shirts in class before we go outside to use the dye. There are lots of ways to tie-dye a shirt, with stripes and spirals and polka dots." She shows us the different techniques, and we get started folding and tying with rubber bands. I decide to do polka dots and take little bunches of my shirt and wrap them up with rubber bands. I also decide to try to talk to Bella again.

"You know, Bella," I say, leaning toward her desk, "I talked to my dad and he said that pink is just really light red, which I think is pretty interesting, don't you?"

"I think pink is just pink," says Bella. She sounds a little grumpy, in my opinion.

"Well, my dad is an artist, so he knows," I say. "You just mix white with red to get pink, so I think people should call pink 'pale red.' Though I don't really see why people like pale colors, anyway. I like bright colors and—"

"I don't care what colors you like, Lola. I like PINK!" says Bella.

"Your face is actually turning a little pale red—I mean pink," I say. That seems to make Bella even madder.

"Don't worry," I say, trying to make

her feel better. "My face turns pale red, too, when I'm playing soccer."

"Soccer is *boring*," Bella says. "That's *my* opinion. Why would anyone want to chase a ball around all day, anyway?"

"Soccer isn't just chasing a ball around!" I say. "And it's a lot better than dancing around in bedroom slippers!"

"They are ballet slippers—I mean shoes, NOT bedroom slippers!" says Bella.

"Is there a problem, girls?" Ms. Garcia asks, walking over to us.

We both shake our heads.

When the class finishes tying up their shirts, Ms. Garcia leads us out onto the grass, where she has set up lots and lots of different squeeze bottles filled with dye. There is blue, red, purple, green, yellow, orange, pink, and black.

"Everyone, put your gloves on!" Ms. Garcia says. "And try *very* hard not to get dye on your clothes."

I pick out orange and blue and start in on my shirt. Makayla and Alyssa both get purple, because they just *have* to do everything alike, and I see Bella get pink, of course. When I finish my shirt, I decide that something's missing. I walk over to the table and pick out the bottle with black dye in it.

"Why not add a little drama?" I ask myself. I guess I'm not watching where I'm going too closely, because while I'm walking back over to my place on the grass, I trip over Juan's foot and fall forward. So does the bottle of dye. Right into Bella's lap, where it not only splashes her tie-dyed shirt but all over her pink skirt, too.

"Lola!" she yells. "You ruined my shirt! And my skirt!"

"Oh no!" I say, and start to get up, reaching out to get the bottle. Bella grabs it first. I take a look at her and watch as she points the bottle straight at my purple tennis shoes.

"Don't even think about it!" I say, and I grab the bottle, too. For a second, nothing happens, but I guess we're squeezing the bottle tight, because all of a sudden the top pops off and there is a big EXPLO-SION of black dye.

Everyone starts yelling, because even though Bella and I are the ones who are dripping with black dye, splatters of it have gone everywhere.

"You ruined our shirts!" says Makayla.

"What's wrong with you?" says Alyssa.

Even Ms. Garcia, the best teacher in the whole wide world, looks upset.

"Lola! Bella! WHAT have you done?" she asks.

"It was her fault," Bella and I say at the very same time, pointing drippy black fingers at each other.

I can tell Ms. Garcia is *not* happy with our answer. Uh-oh, I think. This can mean only one thing…Principal Blot.

Chapter Four
The Moms Meet

Principal Blot takes one look at us and then sends us to the bathroom to clean up as best we can. We stand in front of the sinks and try to wash the dye off our hands and arms, and the sinks fill with black water. I watch Bella try to clean her skirt with water and a paper towel, but it just makes the color spread. I feel pretty bad.

When we finally get back to the main office, I see my mom and a person who must be Ms. Benitez talking to Principal Blot in her office. The door is open, but I can't hear what they are saying.

"Oh no!" Bella says. "She called our moms?"

"Yep," I say. "But don't worry. Principal Blot calls my parents all the time." I don't think that makes Bella feel better, though, because she looks like she's about to cry. I give her back a little pat, like my mom does to me when I'm sad, and she doesn't seem to mind.

After what feels like a long time, Principal Blot comes out and says, "Lola, Bella, come on in."

We walk into the office and take a seat.

"Ms. Garcia explained what happened in class today," Principal Blot says. "Do either of you have something to say?"

I look at Bella.

"I'm sorry about your skirt," I say, "but it was an accident. I tripped."

"It's my favorite," Bella says. "My *abuelita* gave it to me."

"I'm extra sorry, then," I say, and I am.

"I know," Bella says with a sigh. "I'm sorry I squeezed the ink bottle so hard it exploded—I'm very strong because I do ballet."

"Actually, the ink bottle exploded because *I* squeezed it too hard. I play soccer, so I'm even stronger than you," I say.

"Actually," Bella says in a not very quiet voice, "you're wrong. I think—"

"That's enough, Bella," Principal Blot interrupts, looking at each of us, and then our moms. "I think I see the problem." Of course she *sees* the problem, I think. We are both covered in black dye!

"But since you've both apologized and it was *mostly* an accident, you won't be punished. But you do need to get home and change your clothes before com-

ing back to school—that's why I called your moms. We can't have you soaking wet."

We all walk out together, and Ms. Benitez and my mom start talking in Spanish. Bella and I go get our stuff, and when we come back, they're laughing and smiling and exchanging phone numbers. Bella and I look at each other with surprise. Our moms look like they are...

scheming. "Scheming" is a fancy word for making a secret plan.

On the way home, Mom surprises me.

"Maria Benitez and I think you and Bella should get to know each other better," she says. "You might find out you have more in common than you think."

"I already know Bella," I say. "She likes pink and thinks dancers are better than soccer players!"

"Well, we decided that it would be a good experience for each of you to try something new, so you, my darling, are going to attend one of Bella's dance classes, and Bella is coming to one of your soccer practices. You might learn something."

"Are you joking with me?" I ask Mom.

"No, not at all," she says, smiling. I sure don't see what there is to smile about, but I don't tell Mom that.

Dear *Diario,*

So far, this is turning out to be a double-darn cow barn kind of week. Mom doesn't like it when I say "darn," so I usually just say "cow barn," but today I asked her if I could write "darn" if it's just in my *diario,* and she said yes. First, I'm supposed to co-captain the Orange Smoothies with Alyssa, the meanest girl in my school. Second, I don't have anyone to dress like a twin with on Twin Day.

I thought Josh was my super best friend, but I think maybe he's not anymore. I tried ignoring Josh to let him know that my feelings are hurt, but he didn't notice. He just picked me for his soccer team during recess like always. Finally, I got into trouble with a bottle of dye during art. Well, sort of. I had to go to Principal Blot's office again, and now, thanks to my mom and her new best friend, Ms. Benitez, I have to go to a ballet class! Double-darn cow barn.

Shalom,
Lola Levine

Chapter Five
Sharks and Potatoes

Today Bella is going to soccer practice with me. She comes home with me after school so that we can find her some soccer cleats that fit and lend her a pair of my shin guards. She also brings me a bag with a pink leotard and tights in it for her dance class on Saturday. I'm feeling pretty bad about ruining her skirt, so I say sorry one more time.

"That's okay," say Bella, but I'm not sure she means it. We go up to my room.

At first, Bella just stands there, looking at all the things I painted on my wall and ceiling. My room is purple with orange polka dots, and I've got flowers on my closet and stars on my ceiling. Then, she surprises me.

"I like your room, Lola," Bella says, and I see her smile for the very first time.

"Thanks," I say.

"It must be fun to have a dad who's an artist," she says.

"It is," I say. "He's also my soccer

coach." I tell her about soccer and how we have a big game coming up against the Gray Sharks. Bella gets excited.

"Did you know the word 'shark' comes from Mexico, which is where my family is from? It comes from the Mayan word *xok*, which you spell x-o-k, but sounds like the word 'shock,' like an electric shock!" says Bella. "My dad's a professor, and he's always teaching me about Mexican history."

"That's so cool," I say. "I want to shock the Gray Sharks next week," I say, and we both laugh. Bella doesn't even seem nervous when we get to practice, and I'm impressed. She's really good at warm-ups, especially the flamingo—she can lift her heel to her bottom and stand on one leg, no problem.

"Lola," she asks while balancing, "do you like flamingos?"

"Yes!" I say. "They're so cool—they sleep standing up."

"Lola," she says again with a grin, "what COLOR are flamingos?"

"Pink," I say, smiling.

"Maybe you need to change your opinion about pink," Bella says.

"Maybe," I say.

Soccer drills are a lot harder for Bella, and she actually trips a couple of times. I feel bad, but she just gets back up and keeps going. We play a short game, and I tell her to play defense back near me, because then I can give her directions. I think she enjoys that more, especially because our side is winning by one. All of a sudden, Alyssa breaks through the mid-field and is heading straight toward me. The only person between Alyssa and the goal is Bella.

"Go get her!" I yell at Bella. "You can do it!"

"What do I do?" she asks, running toward Alyssa.

"Kick the ball away!" I say, and watch as Bella manages to kick the ball, but then tumbles forward and falls flat on her face in the grass. Coach Berg blows his whistle. The scrimmage is over.

I run out of the goal to check on Bella.

"Are you okay?" I ask, helping her up.

"I think I'll stick to ballet," she says, rubbing the mud stains from her knees and trying to fix her hair. She's covered

in grass. I've never seen Bella wear so much... green, but I decide not to say anything about it.

"Did we win?" she asks.

"Yes!" I say, smiling. "Thanks to you. People always say that it isn't about winning or losing, but what they don't say is that winning is a lot more fun."

"I agree," says Bella.

"I've got an idea," I say. "Let's see if I

can get Dad to take us out for some after-practice french fries. Potatoes come from Peru, you know!"

At school the next day, I write a note to Ms. Garcia.

Dear Ms. Garcia,

I am so sorry about messing up the tie-dye project.

> **Sorry**
> **Oops**
> **Reckless**
> **Really wish I didn't do that**

You are the best teacher in the whole wide world!

Shalom,
Lola Levine

Ms. Garcia hands me a note at the end of the day.

Dear Lola,

Apology accepted. I'm very glad you and Bella are spending time together.

Sincerely,
Ms. Garcia

The night before I'm supposed to go to Bella's ballet class, I have a terrible nightmare. I dream that I'm trying to put on ballet shoes but don't know how to tie up the ribbons and accidently tie my shoes together. When I stand up to dance, I fall flat on my face and all the pink ballerinas laugh at me. It's not just that they are wearing pink costumes, but their hair and faces are pink, too! It's soooo scary! I must be making a lot of noise in my sleep, because the next thing I know, I'm awake and Mom, Dad, and Ben are all in my room. I explain my dream, and they hug me tight. Mom makes me a little chamomile tea with honey, and Ben gives me Chewie to sleep with for the rest of the night. I do sleep a lot better.

Sometimes my little brother, Ben, doesn't bother me at all, not one bit.

Chapter Six
Bravo Ballet

I look into the mirror, and I don't recognize myself. I'm so…pink. I can see why tights are called tights. I feel like I'm wrapped in plastic. My leotard is itchy. Ben pops his head into my room, takes one look at me, and laughs.

"You look funny, Lola!" he says. "Where are the rest of your clothes?"

"Mom!" I yell. "Help!" A couple of seconds later, Mom runs into the room. She's fast.

"Lola, what is it? Is everything okay?" she asks.

"No!" I say. "Look at me! I can't wear these weird clothes."

"Lola, you scared me," she says. "I thought something was really wrong."

"Something IS really wrong," I tell her. "I can't go out of the house like this. I'm practically naked. And I'll be cold. And itchy. This looks like an ugly pink bathing suit."

"Lola," Mom says, "you look lovely. Ballerinas wear clothes that are easy to

move in and that highlight their arms and
legs."

"Why can't I highlight my arms and
legs in my soccer shorts and a T-shirt?"
I ask.

"Well, the teacher needs to see the
exact line of your body as you dance," she

says. "You aren't going to let something as small as clothes stop you from going to Bella's dance class, are you? After all, she went to your soccer practice."

"Okay, Mom," I say, "but can I at least wear soccer shorts over my leotard on the way to the studio?"

"Sure," says Mom. "But you'll have to let me put your hair in a bun. I think I can manage it."

"Fine," I say, and I picture myself with a big cinnamon bun on my head.

Mom drives me to Bella's dance studio, and Ben tags along. He keeps teasing me.

"Lola is going to dance...in her underpants!" he says.

"Ben," I say, "it's a LEOTARD, not underwear!" I'm pretty grumpy when I get out of the car. Mom and I walk in through the glass doors that say BRAVO BALLET ACADEMY in great big pink letters—Ben stays outside with his soccer ball.

I look around the studio. There are lots of girls in leotards, and each one looks the same to me. Bella runs up and surprises me by giving me a big hug.

"I'm so glad you came, Lola! I thought you wouldn't, you know. I like your hair that way!" she says. I reach up to the tiny bun my mom managed to make and look at the big bun on Bella's head. It looks like a giant doughnut.

"Did you know this studio is named after a famous Mexican ballet dancer?" she asks. I shake my head.

"Well, it is! Her name was Guillermina Bravo, and she was amazing."

I smile, but the truth is it feels like monkeys are doing cartwheels in my stomach.

"I'm a little nervous," I tell Bella.

"Don't be!" says Bella, and she introduces me to a bunch of other girls dressed in leotards. One of them is Mira Goldstein.

"Hi, Mira!" I say. I like Mira a lot, even though she's Alyssa's little sister. "Did you see Ben? He's outside."

Mira runs to the front door, opens it, and yells, "Ben, come in! You can watch through the windows!"

"Lola, may we stay and watch?" Mom asks.

"Sure," I say.

Luckily, Ben's on good behavior because

Mira is here. Mira and Ben are best friends. Being best friends with Ben can be a little dangerous because he's pretty wild. Mira is the only girl without a bun. That's because her hair is still growing back from when Ben accidentally cut half of it off after a bubble-gum blowing contest (the gum got stuck in her hair). Her hair is slicked all the way back, though, with some sort of gel or hair spray. Just as I'm about to ask her if I can touch it, Bella grabs my arm.

"Let's go, Lola! Take off your shorts. It's time for class," she says. I do and give Ben a look that says he'd better not tease me, not even once!

We all line up against a wooden bar. I'm right behind Bella.

A teacher walks in and says, "Good afternoon, girls."

"Good afternoon, Mr. Duval," all the ballerinas reply. Then they put one foot in front of the other and bend their knees.

"That's our ballet master, Mr. Duval," says Bella. "You should curtsy."

"Is a curtsy the knee bend you just did?" I ask.

"Yep," Bella replies, and I try it. It isn't too hard.

Mr. Duval opens his mouth and starts giving directions. In French. I don't speak French.

"Two *demi-pliés* and one *grand plié* in first position and full *port de bras* into a forward bend. *Tendu* to second position. *Port de bras*," he says, and the ballerinas in front of me and behind me start moving.

What do these words mean? What are first position and second position? I can't figure it out. Everyone is moving and doing things on the bar but me. I try to copy Bella, though, and Mr. Duval doesn't seem to mind, because he just smiles at me and nods his head. I do figure out the forward, backward, and side bends, and those stretches feel really good.

Later in class, we do something called a *grand jeté*, which is a sort of leap in the air. As a goalie, I'm used to jumping to catch balls, so I'm not horrible at it.

"Bend your knees in a *plié* and take

a deep breath just before you leap," Mr. Duval explains. "Pretend that you are doing the splits on a magic flying carpet!"

I finally get it, and I do a pretty good leap, in my opinion. Mr. Duval agrees.

"Very good!" he says, and I'm so happy that I feel like I can *plié* and *grand jeté* all day. I'm also dripping with sweat. When class is finally over, I tell Bella, "You know, that was a lot harder than I ever thought. I can see why you are so strong."

We walk to the door being held open by Mr. Duval.

"Thank you for letting me come to your class, Mr. Duval," I say, but Mr. Duval isn't looking at me. He's looking out into the lobby.

"Who is that?" Mr. Duval says.

Bella and I take a look, and that's when I see Ben. He's leaping, spinning, and dancing around the lobby. He must have been watching the ballet class very closely through the window, because he seems almost good at it.

"That's my brother, Ben," I tell Mr. Duval. "He's a soccer player."

"No…," says Mr. Duval, "he's a dancer!"

The next thing I know, Mr. Duval is talking to my mom and Ben, asking if Ben might be interested in taking ballet classes or being a guest dancer in one of the performances.

"But a boy can't be a ballerina," says Ben.

"Sure, you can," I say, "you can be a *ballerino.*"

"Actually, you would just be a ballet dancer," says Mr. Duval. "We need more boys, and I can see you have natural talent."

"What do you think, Ben?" asks Mom. "Shall we talk about it at home when you've had time to think about it?"

Ben nods, and Mr. Duval gives Mom a schedule of classes.

"Ben!" says Mira. "You should dance with us! It would be so fun."

Ben looks at Mira.

"Okay," he says, and does a spin.

Chapter Seven
The Big Game

Dear *Diario*,

Tomorrow is our big game against the Gray Sharks. I'm so

excited! I have my soccer uniform folded up next to my bed, with my shoes, shin guards, and lucky headband all ready to go. My mom told me that she invited Bella and her mom to the soccer game. Afterward, we are all going out to lunch.

I think it is nice that Mom has a new friend. It turns out she and Ms. Benitez have a lot in common. They both came to the United States from Latin America when they were teenagers, only Ms. Benitez and her family came from Mexico. Ms. Benitez doesn't write for a newspaper, but she does write poems.

Besides, I'm starting to like Bella a lot. Why can't a ballerina and a soccer player be friends?

Shalom,
Lola Levine

On the way to the game, Ben tells me a joke.

"What type of dance does a polar bear go to?"

"I don't know, Ben," I say, groaning.

"A snow ball!" he says, grinning from ear to ear.

When we get to the soccer field, I realize I have a big problem. I can't find my lucky headband! It's orange, and I wear it for every game. I run over to Mom. She's standing with Ben, Ms. Benitez, and Bella.

"Help!" I say. "I've lost my lucky head-band! What should I do?"

"Can't you borrow one from a team-mate? Someone should have an extra."

"But, Mom," I say, "you don't understand. This is my SPECIAL headband. I haven't lost a game while wearing it."

"Sweetheart, you haven't lost because you and your team have played well," Mom answers.

"I've got an idea," says Bella, pulling her long pink ribbon out of her hair. "Use this! It's lucky, too." She then ties it around my hair and makes a bow. A bow. Ugh. I want to take it off, but Bella looks happy that she's able to help, so I decide not to. I also decide not to tell Bella my opinion of bows, because I know it will hurt her feelings. Instead, I just say thanks.

Then I've got to run to the field. It's game time. We do great, even though Alyssa smirks and points at the bow in my hair, whispering something to the other forward. I don't have time to get annoyed because I'm too busy playing my very best.

With two minutes to go, we are ahead by one. Oh no! One of my defenders fouls someone. It's a penalty kick, which means the soccer ball is coming directly at me. I need to stop one more goal if we are going to win. The referee blows the whistle, and one of the Sharks players runs toward the ball and kicks it toward the middle-right side of my net. I leap, and remember Mr. Duval's advice—do splits on a magic carpet! Sure enough, I stop the ball with my pointed toe, kicking it out. My team

cheers, and I am so relieved. Thanks, Mr. Duval, I think. And Bella, too.

After the game, I return Bella's pink bow. Just then, Alyssa walks up to us.

"I can't believe you're friends with Lola," Alyssa says to Bella. "She's so weird."

"Well," Bella says, "I guess I'm weird, too. After all, I only wear clothes that are pink—I mean pale red." We laugh, but Alyssa doesn't get it. Still, Alyssa is my co-captain, and she worked as hard on the field as anyone else.

"Good game," I say to Alyssa. "You played great."

"Thanks," she says, and stomps off, but not before I hear her say, "You too."

"Lola," Bella says, "do you want to be twins for Twin Day?"

"I sure do!" I say, and I mean it.

Later, when Mom tucks me into bed, I tell her, "I guess your ballet *scheme* worked."

"I guess so," Mom says, smiling. "But only because you were willing to try to learn something new." Then she gives me a kiss on the cheek and turns off the light.

Chapter Eight
Twin Day

"I wonder where Ms. Garcia is?" I ask Josh as he, Bella, and I walk into the second-grade classroom.

"I can't wait for her to see our outfits," I say. Bella and I are wearing pink tutus and orange shirts we made that say A GRAND JETÉ A DAY KEEPS THE GOALS AWAY!!! We also have on orange-striped tube socks (luckily, I have more than one pair of Orange Smoothies socks). We're wearing pink and orange nail polish, and we've braided our hair the same way, even though my braids are short and Bella's are long.

"You look cool!" Josh says. He and Juan are wearing matching baseball shirts, hats, and jeans.

"So do you," I say with a smile.

"Want to play soccer at recess?" Josh asks. I think he's worried that I might not want to, since I'm dressed in a tutu.

"Of course!" I say. I know that Bella doesn't like playing soccer, but just because we're friends doesn't mean we have to do everything the same, right? Still, it's pretty fun to have a twin on Twin Day.

"Besides," I say, "I have a new trick to show you about leaping toward the ball."

"Did you learn it at soccer practice this week?" Juan asks.

"Nope," I say. "I learned it at ballet."

"What?!" Josh and Juan say at the exact same time. I just laugh.

Before I go home, I leave an acrostic

in Bella's cubby—I know she'll see it first thing tomorrow morning.

> **B**allerina
> **E**legant
> **L**oyal
> **L**oves pink
> **A**miga (This means "friend" in Spanish, but you know that, and I do, too!)

Dear *Diario*,

Guess what? This weekend I'm going to my very first slumber party ever. I'm going to Bella Benitez's house, and I'm bringing my own nail polish, because all her colors are shades of pink, of course. I can't wait. Bella says that we are going to have a special breakfast with *pan dulce* that we'll make ourselves! I've had Mexican sweet bread before, but I've never made it. I can't wait to make all the special shapes—ears and shells and piggies to dip in warm milk!

I also learned that my mom is almost always right. Trying new things isn't so bad, even if it means wearing a pink leotard and making my hair into a cinnamon bun.

Shalom,
Lola Levine